j
P
W

923-1574

Wild, Margaret

The queens holiday

DATE DUE

	DATE DUE		
JUN 2 9 201			
JAN 0 4 2012			
JUN 1 3 2012			
MAR 1 9 2014			
APR 1 6 2014			09
			09

GAYLORD
M2

The QUEEN'S HOLIDAY

by MARGARET WILD

illustrated by SUE O'LOUGHLIN

Orchard Books • New York

Text copyright © 1992 by Margaret Wild. Illustrations copyright © 1992 by Sue O'Loughlin.
First American edition 1992 published by Orchard Books. First published in Australia by Penguin Books Australia Ltd.

Orchard Books, 95 Madison Avenue, New York, NY 10016

Manufactured in the United States of America. Printed by Barton Press, Inc. Bound by Horowitz/Rae
Book design by Mina Greenstein
The text of this book is set in 18 pt. ITC Gamma Book.   10   9   8   7   6   5   4   3   2   1

Library of Congress Cataloging-in-Publication Data
Wild, Margaret, date.   The queen's holiday / by Margaret Wild ; illustrated by Sue O'Loughlin. — 1st American ed.   p.   cm.
Summary: When the Queen and her entourage go to the beach, the Queen takes charge in no uncertain fashion.
ISBN 0-531-05973-1.   ISBN 0-531-08573-2 (lib. bdg.)
[1. Kings, queens, rulers, etc.—Fiction.   2. Beaches—Fiction.]   I. O'Loughlin, Sue, ill.   II. Title.   PZ7.W64574Qe   1992
[E]—dc20   91-14024

The QUEEN'S HOLIDAY

One terribly hot day the Queen said,
"Let's all go down to the sea to cool off."

When they were ready to go, the Queen followed the butler,
who carried all the food for the morning tea.

The page boy carried the swimming costumes.
The lady-in-waiting carried the royal potty.

The bodyguard carried the guns.

The groom carried the corgi dogs.
The doctor carried the medicine bag.

The palace guard carried the jewels.
The maids carried the pillows.

And the footman carried the suitcases,
the day the Queen went on holiday.

But it was a long, long walk to the seaside,

and on the way everyone got rather hot and silly.

The footman tossed the suitcases into a fish pond.
The maids had a pillow fight.

The palace guard ran off with the jewels.
The doctor poured the Queen's cough mixture into a flower bed.

The dogs were chased by an alley cat.
The bodyguard shot himself in the foot.

The lady-in-waiting made mud pies with the royal potty,
and the page boy tied the swimming costumes into a jump rope.

And the butler ate *all* the morning tea,
the day the Queen went on holiday.

"This simply will not do!" exclaimed the Queen.

The Queen fished out the suitcases,

stuffed the feathers back into the pillows,

caught the palace guard,
bought another bottle of cough mixture, and rescued the dogs.

She bandaged the bodyguard's foot,

rinsed the royal potty,

unknotted the swimming costumes,

and scolded the butler.

"What a greedy pig," said the Queen.
"Now let's all get going before I really get angry."

Then the Queen marched everyone,
one–two, down to the sea,

and there they stayed having a wonderful time until...

the bell rang for afternoon tea—
the day the Queen went on holiday.